HOME FRONT HEROES

W
FRANKLIN WATTS
LONDON•SYDNEY

This edition first published in 2005 by
Franklin Watts
338 Euston Road
London
NW1 3BH

Franklin Watts Australia
Level 17 / 207 Kent Street
Sydney
NSW 2000

Editors: Kyla Barber, Paula Borton, Suzy Jenvey
Designers: Jason Anscomb, Kirstie Billingham
Cover illustration: Andy Hammond
Consultant: Dr Anne Millard, BA Hons, Dip Ed, PhD

A CIP catalogue record for this book
is available from the British Library.

ISBN 0 7496 6317 0

Dewey Classification 823.914

Printed in Great Britain

HOME FRONT HEROES

Contents

Sid's War

by
Jon Blake
Illustrations by Kate Sheppard

1

Evacuate!

It was Swotty Joan who found the labels. Buster Biggs pushed her in the stock cupboard when Mr Fisher was out of the classroom. When she came out she was holding up a square of linen with my name on it: SIDNEY KELLY.

"There's a big pile of them!" she said.

Swotty Joan was right. Hidden on a back shelf was a whole stack of labels, two for everyone in the class.

"What are these for?" I asked.

At that moment there was a roar from behind us. Mr Fisher was back, and he wasn't happy.

"Those labels are nothing to do with you!" he snapped.

"But, sir," I protested. "They've got our names on them."

Mr Fisher told me not to be cheeky,

even though I wasn't, and then backed down and explained.

"As you know," he said, "there is *not* going to be a war. But, *just in case*, the school is making plans to evacuate you."

It was the first time I'd heard the word EVACUATE. I didn't know what it meant but it sent my blood cold. EVACUATE. It sounded a bit like EVAPORATE. If you evaporate it means you turn into gas. Everyone said the Germans were going to gas us, which was why we all had big rubber gas masks.

I looked up the word EVACUATE in a dictionary:

Evacuate:

1. Move people away from a place of danger.

2. Empty the bowels.

So EVACUATE had two meanings! But which one was Mr Fisher on about? I needed answers fast.

"Sir," I asked. "Are we going to take it in turns to evacuate?"

"No, Sidney," replied Mr Fisher. "We are all going to evacuate together."

"Even the teachers?" I asked.

"Even the teachers," replied Mr Fisher.

"Sir," I asked. "Where are we going to evacuate?"

"Into the country," replied Mr Fisher.

I still wasn't too sure what Mr Fisher meant, but I found out soon enough. Next

day there was a meeting in the church hall
and a man gave a speech. He said that if
a war *did* start (even though it wouldn't,
of course) important cities were going to
get bombed. So it would be a good idea if
all the children and blind people and
mums-with-babies got out quickly.

Dad had signed a form to say they
could take me and my sister Rita. I was
going to be torn away from Mum, Dad,

Gran and, even worse, my cat Tiger. Ah well, I thought. It was pretty bad, but not as bad as emptying your bowels in a field.

2

The Real Thing

Over the next weeks we started practising for this EVACUATION. We were put in teams of fifty and trained to march together and cross roads in an orderly manner. This wasn't easy when you had Buster Biggs swinging his gas mask at your

head. We had to carry our masks in cardboard boxes hung round our necks, and one day we all had to put them on. They were heavy and stuffy and stank of rubber, but at least they hid Buster's face.

Everybody had a haversack. Dad made ours out of old coal sacks. Every week Mum packed them with spare clothes and soap and towels and food for the journey. I don't know why, because we never went anywhere – just round the school yard or down to the railway station and back.

The summer holidays arrived, the weather was brilliant, Dad got called up to the army reserve and we forgot all about leaving London.

But we were in for a surprise. At the end of August we were called back to school and told to go home and pack. This time it was for real.

I didn't sleep much that night. I was even awake when the bugs came out of the wallpaper and climbed up in bed with me.

In the morning I said goodbye to Tiger.

"I won't forget you, Tiger," I said.

"You're right there," said Rita. "Have you smelt your raincoat?"

I rushed to the door and grabbed my one and only coat. It stank. Tiger

had been marking his
territory again.

"Mum!" I cried.
"The cat's peed on my
coat! Do something!"

"Too bad," said
Mum. "You've got
to be in school in
five minutes."

Mum wasn't
the kind of
person to
get all
tearful about
her kiddies
leaving home.

Some of the other mums, though, they were crying and wailing and going, "Oh my babies!" all the way to school.

We lined up in the playground behind two kids carrying a sign with our school numbers on it. There was a check of names, gas masks and haversacks. Then we were off, marching like soldiers, with a big trail of crying mums keeping to the rear.

Yes, we kept pretty good order, apart from one small problem. No one wanted to walk next to me.

"Sir!" wailed Robert Goody. "Sid stinks!"

"KEEP IN LINE!" barked Mr Fisher. "WE DON'T WANT AN ACCIDENT!"

"Sid's already had one," mumbled Kevin Palmer.

When we finally arrived at the
station, it was one great seething mass of
school kids, all labelled and haversacked
and grey-faced with anxiety. It was hard
to believe all these children were going to
find new homes. *Were* there that many
houses in the country? Were there *any*
houses in the country? I'd never been

further than our aunty's house in Hackney.

I'd never been on a train, either, and when I saw that great steaming monster I felt a mixture of utter terror and fantastic excitement. All around, mums were saying their last goodbyes, and as I boarded the train I caught sight of my own mum, waving frantically. As I waved back, she

began to cry.

I'd never seen that one before. I wondered if she knew something I didn't.

"Sir," I asked Mr Fisher as the train pulled away, "if there isn't going to be a war, why are ten thousand kids leaving London?"

"What *are* you talking about?" replied Mr Fisher impatiently. "Of course there's going to be a war!"

"Oh," I said. "That's all right then."

I settled back and stared out of the train

window. Parts of London I'd never seen, houses ten times bigger than our little terrace, then fields, trees, and . . . animals! Herds of animals!

"Look, Rita!" I said. "What

are those?"

Rita, who was trying to sit as far away from me as possible, glanced out of the window.

"Cows, stupid," she said.

"How do you know?"

"From an old book of nursery rhymes."

"Oh," I said. "Do you think they can really jump?"

"Eh?"

"You know, like over the moon."

Rita screwed up her face. "Have we really got to stay together?" she groaned.

3

Mrs Brown-Hat

The journey took hours and hours. The teachers told us when to eat our packed lunches but they couldn't tell us about where we'd be staying. They didn't know any more than we did.

At last we pulled into a station. A

dozen old buses were waiting in the gathering evening gloom. One of these took us down a narrow country lane and into a mysterious village with not much more than a church and a few houses. The bus stopped and they took us into the village

hall, which was a bare and dismal place with the windows blacked out. That worried me. The reason for the blackout was so the enemy bombers couldn't see, but the enemy bombers weren't supposed to come here, were they?

Anyway, we were lined up and told to look our best. A man called the EVACUATION WARDEN told us to KEEP OUR CHINS UP and LOOK SPRUCE. Then the doors opened and in came the villagers. They strolled around looking us up and down, some trying to be chatty, others whispering behind their hands. I pulled my sleeves down to cover the bug bites, and tried to smile. But I wasn't smiling inside. I felt like a bit of rubbish at a jumble sale.

One by one, my friends got picked off and taken away. Not me though. Every time someone came near they took one good sniff and moved quickly along.

By and by, a short, stocky woman came into the hall. She had a rough red face, a friendly smile, and dirty gumboots. I heard her tell the man in charge she was looking for four youngsters to help her out on the farm. Immediately Buster Biggs stuck out his chest and put on the most pathetic goody-goody smile.

Imagine my horror when she went straight up and picked him.

Worse was to follow. The red-faced woman chose three more kids, and one of them was my sister.

"But we're together!" I blurted out, but no one seemed to hear.

The red-faced woman led her new family from the hall, chatting about horses, a motherly arm around Rita's shoulder.

I felt very alone.

More villagers arrived, more kids departed. Soon there were just four of us.

Then three.
Then two.
Then me.

And all the villagers were gone.

"Oh dear," said the evacuation warden. "I did think there were billets for all of you. There's always *someone* who lets you down."

Just at that moment the door at the back of the hall flew open. A tall, stiff woman marched in, wearing a tweed suit and brown hat topped off with a feather.

"George!" she cried.
"*Do* forgive me!
We've had a terrible
hoo-hah at the
Women's Institute
and my timetable
is ruined!"

My innards
shrank. Mrs Brown-Hat
turned sharply towards
me. Her face dropped.

"Is this all that's
left?" she asked.

"I'm afraid so,
Jessica," replied the warden.

Mrs Brown-Hat's eyes flashed me
up and down, cold and hard as a till.
"Oh," she said. She moved closer, and
I think she was about to ask my name,

when a wave of shock and horror went over her face.

"What is that *dreadful* smell?" she cried.

"Cat's pee," I blurted out.

"Cat's *what*!?" cried Mrs Brown-Hat, even more shocked and horrified.

"We could ask Mr Porter if he could take another boy," blabbed the warden hurriedly.

"Not. At. All!" snapped Mrs Brown-Hat. "I shall make it my *personal crusade* to give this boy a carbolic bath, and when I've done with that I'll wash his mouth out for good measure!"

4

The Enemy

Mrs Brown-Hat, whose real name was Mrs Abbott, lived in a house called Orchard Cottage. I never knew houses had names, but then I'd never seen a house like Mrs Abbott's. It had its own gate and a front garden big enough to build another house in. There was an entrance hall which was as big as a room in itself, a sitting room, a dining room, a kitchen, a pantry, a room they called The Study, not to mention the bedrooms. There was even a bathroom and an indoor wc, which Mrs Abbot called The Lavatory. The whole place smelled of lavender, and everything was in such perfect order I was almost scared to breathe.

Mrs Abbott wasn't joking about the carbolic bath. Not only that, she checked my hair for lice and made me change. Then I had to take my coat into the

garage, where there was a real motor car, just sitting there, with a real Mr Abbott polishing the bonnet. He didn't say much, but with Mrs Abbott around, that wasn't surprising.

"I can't understand why he didn't wear another coat," said Mrs Abbott.

"Haven't got another coat," I mumbled.

"Yes, and I expect your father spends all his wages on beer," replied Mrs Abbott.

Next, I was shown to my room, except it wasn't called my room. It was called Colin's Room. Colin's ties were still in the wardrobe, and Colin's photo was in pride of place on the dressing table. Colin was away flying planes in the airforce, and, according to Mrs Abbott, he was the most perfect human being who ever lived. I

was not to move a thing in Colin's bedroom, and WOE BETIDE ME if there was the tiniest scratch on the furniture.

I went to bed that night the most miserable person on earth. I'd never slept in a room on my own before, and suddenly

I ached to be back with Mum, Dad, Gran and Rita, in a house full of noise and life. Downstairs the only sound came from the wireless, followed by Mrs Abbott getting angry about Hitler. I'd never met Hitler, but I had met Mrs Abbott, and as far as I was concerned *she* was the enemy.

5

Dream Cake!

Two days later it was Sunday 3rd
September. Mr and Mrs Abbott took me
to church and Britain declared war on
Germany. My spirits sank when I heard
that news. Now I would never go home, I
thought. But Mrs Abbott's spirits were on
fire. She said ENGLAND EXPECTS

EVERY MAN TO DO HIS DUTY, and
gave me a huge long list of jobs to do, as if
I was her servant.

I trudged through the day feeling
like the whole thing was a bad dream.
Mrs Abbott went visiting and Mr Abbott
practised his golf swing in the garden,
always with one eye on me. Then, just as
my stomach was starting to rumble, Mrs
Abbott came back. Under her arm was
a box. She opened the box and lifted out
THE CAKE OF MY DREAMS.

It was a dark, rich fruit cake with big swollen cherries busting out of the sides. On top was a layer of marzipan as thick as your wrist, and on top of that was white icing decorated with red and blue sugar flowers.

"This should cause a stir when the vicar visits," said Mrs Abbott.

She cast an anxious glance at me as she carried the cake into the pantry. Then

she went to the kitchen cabinet, took out
a key, locked the pantry door, glanced
at me again, and checked the door for
good measure.

On Monday we started school again.
We were back in our old classes, with our
old teachers, except we were crammed into
the hall of the village school.

The moment she saw me, Rita
rushed up to me. She was beaming all
over her face.

"We're having a *brilliant* time!" she
said. "Mrs Bosley lets us help out
with the
animals,

and I milked a cow on Saturday, and we
all sit in the kitchen and eat great big
home-made pies, and play games, and Mr
Bosley plays a fiddle!"

I tried to smile.
"What's your
house like?"

I was just
about to answer
when Buster Biggs
barged in. "Met
any *yokels* yet?"
he said. "Oo ar,
oi lives in the
country, oi do!"

"Oh shut up, Buster!" said Rita.
"You're ruining it for every one, you are!"

"You should come down the farm,
Sid!" said Buster. "Chase some piggies!
Hear 'em squeal!"

"I'll make you squeal," said Rita.

Buster ignored her. "What's your house like, Smelly Kelly?" he asked.

"Brilliant," I replied.

"Oh yeah," said Buster doubtfully.

"Got my own room," I said.

Buster frowned. "Your own room?" he said. "You lucky dog! I've got to share with two stupid yokels."

"And there's other things," I said.

"Like what?" asked Buster.

"Like . . . cake," I replied.

"We get cake," said Buster.

"Not like this cake," I said.

"Why?" said Buster. "What's so special about it?"

I just smiled.

6

Under Curfew

We all planned to meet up that evening, down at the river. Jimmy Nolan had got a big bottle of ginger beer, and Buster reckoned we could catch fish using a stick and a pair of cotton stockings. I was just looking forward to spending some time with my mates.

But I was in for a big disappointment. After we'd had tea (which Mrs Abbott called 'dinner'), Mrs Abbott told me I was to tidy Colin's room.

"But I'm meeting my sister!" I protested.

Mrs Abbott was outraged. "You do not leave this house without my permission!" she said. "And till school starts tomorrow you are UNDER CURFEW."

I told her that Mum never put me UNDER CURFEW, whatever that meant.

Mrs Abbott told me that while I was under her roof SHE WAS THE LAW.

"There's a war on now," she reminded me. "And we must all make sacrifices."

Maybe we could sacrifice *you*, I thought to myself.

Next day at school, no one could understand why I didn't go to the river.

"It was brilliant!" said Buster. "I was chucking stones at the fishes, and I got one right on the back."

"Yeh, that's

why the farmer chased us off," said Rita.

"Stupid yokel," said Buster. "So where were you, Sid?"

"Me?" I replied. " I had better things to do."

"Such as?"

"You couldn't even imagine."

Buster began to look frustrated. "Tell us," he said.

Mr Fisher rang the school bell.

"It's that cake," mumbled Buster, but I was already on my way to lessons.

7

Sinful Creature

That evening Mrs Abbott had an important committee meeting. She was on lots of COMMITTEES, like the FRIENDS OF ST MARY'S CHURCH COMMITTEE, the WOMEN'S INSTITUTE COMMITTEE, the EVACUATION COMMITTEE, and

the RAT GASSING COMMITTEE. No,
actually, I made the last one up. It's just
that Mrs Abbott is *obsessed* with rats, like
she's obsessed with lice, ringworm,
bedbugs and everything she thinks lives in
my underpants.

Anyway, this committee was meeting
in the next village which meant Mr Abbott
had to drive her. Mrs Abbott thought
about taking me along, but I think she
would have been ashamed to be seen with
me. So she left me alone, with the usual

list of jobs, and a SOLEMN PLEDGE to
be on my VERY BEST BEHAVIOUR.

I don't think I'd ever been alone in
a house before, let alone a mansion like
Mrs Abbott's. It wasn't long before I
started prying into all the corners I wasn't
allowed. I went in the study and I went
in Mrs Abbott's bedroom. Then I
prowled through the kitchen and my
eyes fell on the pantry door.

I could just *try* it, I suppose . . .

Blimey!

I couldn't believe it!

She'd *forgotten to lock it!*

Without a second thought, I picked up the cake carried it carefully into the kitchen and laid it on the table. My eyes feasted on its dark secrets. I brought my nose close to the glistening icing and drew a deep luxurious breath.

There was a knock at the door.

I jumped back.

Another knock.

I ran to the window and looked out. There at the door stood Buster Biggs.

"Sid!" he said, seeing me. "Let us in, will you?"

I opened the door. Buster walked straight in and looked around. "Wow," he said. "Posh, eh? Better than our dump."

"What do you want?" I asked.

"Just visiting my mate!" Buster replied. "So . . . where's this cake?"

"Ah," I said. "So that's it."

I led Buster through to the kitchen. His eyes nearly popped out of his head. "She made that for *you*?" he exclaimed.

"Sure," I said.

Buster sank into a chair, elbows on the table, panting like a dog.

"Gi'us a slice," he said.

"No," I replied.

"Gi'us a slice," he repeated.

"Can't," I replied.

"Course you can," replied Buster. "It's your cake."

"I'm saving it," I said.

"What for?"

"The end of the war."

" But that won't be for *weeks*!"

Buster jumped from his chair, opened a kitchen drawer, and handed me a knife.

"If that's your cake," he said slowly,

"cut me a slice *now*."

I was trapped.

"OK," I said quietly.

As if in a dream, I saw myself slicing into Mrs Abbott's precious cake, handing the piece I'd cut to Buster, and watching him push the dark sticky mass into his face.

"Mm-glovely," he grunted, spitting crumbs all over me. "Aren't you having some?"

"Sure," I said. I watched myself cut another slice, and this time feed my own face. Just as Buster said, it was glovely.

"Cheerio, pal," said Buster. "See you tomorrow."

With that he upped and left. I sat there in a daze, unable to believe what I'd just done, but telling myself it was only fair. Why *should* people like Mrs Abbott have the luxuries while we had the scraps?

We were supposed to be on the same side!

My thoughts were interrupted by the sound of a car engine. In a blind panic, I packed the cake back into the pantry, covered it with a cloth, wiped the table and ran upstairs to my bedroom. As if any of that would do any good.

For the next hour things were strangely quiet – just the twitter of conversation and the sound of the news on the radio. Then, suddenly, there was this almighty scream. Footsteps thundered up the stairs. The door flew open and there stood Mrs Abbott as I'd never seen her before. Her face was a pale purple, her eyes were bloodshot and her lips were drawn back like a mad dog's.

"You . . ." she snarled, "you . . . *sinful creature!*"

I backed into the corner of the room. Mrs Abbott pressed in on me.

"A thief!" she railed. "A thief under my roof . . . in *Colin's room*!"

I curled into a ball. Mrs Abbott got wilder still.

"You will suffer for this!" she cried. "Tomorrow morning . . . you will see . . . I shall make you *very sorry*, young man! *Very sorry indeed*!"

Mrs Abbott towered right over me.

"Well?" she snapped. "Have you got anything to say for yourself?"

"Please, Mrs Abbott," I murmured, "I think I've evacuated."

8

A reward

That night I wrote a secret letter to my mum, saying that if anything was to happen to me please look after Tiger, and how sorry I was for breaking the teapot. I didn't know what Mrs Abbott might do to me, but she'd already told me what she would do to the Germans, and it wasn't very nice. I was prepared for anything.

Not a word was spoken at breakfast. Mr Abbott stayed hidden behind his *Daily Telegraph*, and Mrs Abbott's face was like stone.

Then, when it was time for school, Mrs Abbott handed me my haversack with all my belongings in it, grabbed me by the wrist, and frogmarched me through the village. She did not stop marching till she was in the playground, where she waited till the bell had been rung and we had all lined up. Then she marched me to the front and faced Mr Fisher.

"This boy," she said, "has committed an UNPARDONABLE CRIME. As a result I am punishing him . . . by banishing him from my house!"

I couldn't believe it! This wasn't a punishment, it was a reward!

Mr Fisher, however, shook his head.

"But we have nowhere else to put him," he said, "unless, of course, someone would be willing to swap places with him."

Mrs Abbott's steely eyes turned on

the crowd. Everyone seemed to take one step back.

"Would, er, anyone be willing to swap homes with Sidney?" asked Mr Fisher, doubtfully.

Suddenly an arm at the back shot up. "Me, sir!" came a cry.

I strained my eyes.

The arm was attached to none other than my great mate, Buster Biggs.

Mrs Abbott smiled. Buster Biggs smiled. But neither of them smiled quite as widely as me.

Evacuation

To try and cut down on the senseless loss of life during wartime, the government asked people who were not actively involved in the war to move out of the big cities and towns - the targets of the German bombs - and to stay in the countryside where it was safer.

More people were moved during the Second World War (1939-1945) than at any time in British history. Three and a half million were evacuated in the first twelve days of September 1939; by the end of the war the figure was more than four million.

Who was evacuated?

There were three categories of evacuees: schoolchildren between 5 and 15; pregnant women and women with small children; and blind and disabled people. Most of the schoolchildren went in school groups and were accompanied by their teachers.

London was not the only city to be evacuated. Many large cities including Birmingham, Manchester and Glasgow were also evacuated, as were ports such as Southampton and Portsmouth.

The cost of evacuation

The government paid 3 shillings per week for the upkeep of each evacuee. The evacuee's family was required to pay another 6 shillings.

No one was forced to evacuate. Many families chose to stay put – far more than the government had expected. City schools which had been closed down were forced to open again. Also, almost half of the first batch of evacuees had returned home by early 1940.

A second mass evacuation began at Easter 1940, amid fears of a German invasion. To encourage people, the government now paid £1 4s 2d (about £1.21) for each evacuee's keep. It became compulsory to accept evacuees, which created considerable difficulties for poorer country people in small houses.

Experiences and benefits

The experiences of evacuees were many and varied. Some, for example, did not live in houses, but in camps. Others, like Rita in this story, were luckier, and stayed in comfortable homes. In spite of being away from their families and friends, these evacuees had a better experience. In fact, some evacuees liked the country areas so much that they stayed on there after the war – though they weren't always made welcome.

One result of evacuation was that more people were made aware of the vast differences between the classes in British society. Better-off country people saw clearly for the first time the scale of poverty in the cities, together with the bugs and diseases this brought. Working-class people from the towns soon realised that the land they were fighting for was not really theirs, and that they would still be living in the same poor conditions after the war.

This new awareness led many people to demand better living and working conditions when the war ended. In a small victory for women, many men, left behind in the cities, learnt what it was like to do the domestic chores.

The Sandbag Secret

by
Jon Blake

Illustrations by Martin Remphry

1

The Secret Cabinet

It stood in the corner of the room. Just a cheap wooden cabinet, two foot wide by three foot tall. It was there when I came back from the country after being evacuated.

The cabinet was owned by my Uncle Sandy, who had taken over my room while

I was away. I had never seen him open it and there was always a padlock on the door.

We called Uncle Sandy *Uncle Sandbag* because that's what he was like. Short, round and difficult to budge. You could sometimes fire questions at him all day and you wouldn't get an answer.

Well, I was determined to get one answer. I was determined to find out what was in that cabinet.

It was September 1940. Around our table sat seven people – Mum, Dad, me (Billy), my sister Ruby, my brother Roy, Grandad, and Uncle Sandbag.

"What's for tea, Mum?" I asked, cheerfully.

"Woolton Pie," replied Mum.

My heart sank.

"Not Woolton Pie again!" I groaned.

"Shut up and eat what you're given," said Dad.

We'd had some weird food since rationing started. Dried egg omelettes, soya bean dumplings, and this stuff which looked like meat, tasted of fish, and turned out to be whale. None was quite as bad as Woolton Pie, which was made of parsnips, turnips and other things so disgusting they had to be hidden under pastry.

Not that we had better food before the war. Dad was unemployed and we lived in the poorest part of London, the East End. Things were always hard for us.

"I'll have the boy's pie if he doesn't want it," said Uncle Sandbag.

"I *do* want it!" I cried quickly.

That was typical of Uncle Sandbag. The government had a campaign called Dig for Victory which encouraged people to grow their own veg. Uncle Sandbag had his own campaign called Pig for Victory, which involved eating everyone else's food and never sharing his own.

"What did your sister say in her letter, Mildred?" asked Dad.

"She says Portsmouth's had a terrible pounding," replied Mum.

"Do you think they'll bomb London?" asked Ruby, nervously.

"Not unless they're mad!" I said. I told everyone what Gassy Cook had told me. London's air defences were unbeatable – fighter planes, anti-aircraft guns, barrage balloons, you name it.

"But Hitler *is* mad," said Ruby.

"We should never have bombed Berlin," said Grandad.

That was typical of Grandad. Always questioning what the government did.

Grandad used to be a big union man down the docks and Mum said he was red in tooth and claw, whatever that meant.

After tea Ruby went off for her night shift at the weapons factory. Mum sent me on a mission down the road to borrow some cocoa from Mrs Frost.

On the way I passed a new poster by the corner shop.

LOOK OUT - THERE'S A SPY ABOUT.

I studied this poster a long time. The picture showed a man who looked like an ordinary city gent. He didn't have a peculiar hat or funny moustache and he didn't carry a bomb. In other words, he could be anybody. That was a worrying thought.

When I got back from my walk I went up to my room to find Uncle Sandbag struggling with his socks.

"Get these off for me,
will you, Billy?" he said.

"Do I have to?" I replied.

Uncle Sandbag's feet would have
knocked out a gorilla. I don't know why
they stank so bad. Maybe it was the long
walks he went on every day. No one knew
exactly where he went, or what he did.
Uncle Sandbag just said he had "business".

I squatted down by Uncle Sandbag's feet. Then I had a great idea. I took the gas mask out of my shoulder bag and put it on.

Uncle Sandbag didn't see the funny side at all.

"You won't laugh," he said, "when you're using that mask for real."

Uncle Sandbag sounded very sure of this. It was as if he knew something that the rest of us didn't.

2

The Sirens Sound

Next day was Saturday, the 7th of
September. It started like any other day.
We did some queuing, then some more
queuing, then a bit more queuing.

Shopping in wartime was a real pain.
Once I suggested to Dad that we should

buy things off the black market, but he went mad. Only scum dealt on the black market, he said, when everyone else was doing without.

Anyway, that afternoon, when the shopping was done, there came a sound we had hoped never to hear – the wail of the air-raid sirens.

For a while we just stood, staring at the calm afternoon sky, wondering if there'd been a mistake. Then we had the shock of our lives. Over in the east, the sky was turning black with German bombers.

"Inside!" hissed Dad.

The next few hours were the most frightening of my life. The whole family crouched beneath the dinner table, with a mattress on top and armchairs overturned around the sides.

Outside it sounded like the end of the world – an endless racket of explosions and anti-aircraft fire, most of it so close we jumped for shock.

"Why don't they go and bomb the rich?" growled Grandad.

Eventually there was a break in the bombing. We looked out to see that several of the houses in our street had been hit, and the whole landscape was lit by the fearsome glow of the burning docks.

But it wasn't over yet. The docks made a lovely bright beacon for the night bombers, and soon we were crouched back under the table, more terrified than ever. Only Grandad remained calm.

"Of course," he said, in his best story-telling voice, "I remember the *last* time we had Nazis in the East End."

"What?" I said. "Hitler's been here before?"

"Not Hitler," said Grandad. "These were British Nazis. Except they weren't really Nazis. They were called the British Union of Fascists and they were led by a man called Mosley."

"The blackshirts," chimed Dad. "I remember them."

"What happened to them?" I asked.

"We sent them packing," said Grandad.

"Wow!" I said. "Was there a fight?"

"You could say that," said Grandad. "Half the East End turned out to kick their backsides. Mosley made it as far as Cable Street, then we broke through the police lines, and all hell let loose. It was the beginning of the end for Mosley."

"Are there any of these Nazis still about?" I asked, nervously.

"Most got locked up when the war started," replied Grandad. "But I dare say there's still a few roaming free."

I suddenly became aware of Uncle Sandbag's foot nudging me in my ribs. He had gone very quiet. Even in the gloom I could see the cagey look on his face.

3

In Search of a Spy

There was no doubt in my mind now. Uncle Sandbag was a Nazi. I could just imagine him in one of those black shirts, goose-stepping like we'd seen in the newsreels.

And if Uncle Sandbag was a Nazi, it was a dead cert that he was also. . . a spy!

So that's what this "business" was all about! Spying on the British defences, then radioing back to Germany!

But where did he keep his radio set? Of course! The bedroom cabinet!

I made up my mind to follow Uncle Sandbag next day. If I could stop him, I reckoned I might just save London.

The moment Uncle Sandbag set off, I followed on my bicycle, a safe distance behind. The stench of burning rubber and God-knows-what was still hanging in the air. Destruction was everywhere, and most of it was just ordinary people's homes. Rescue workers still sifted through the rubble, looking dog-tired and filthy.

Uncle Sandbag was a man with a mission. He strode out like a marching soldier, casting glances left and right, but never hesitating for a moment.

He turned into a side street. I hurried after,
then jammed on the brakes. The street had
been cordoned off
because of an
unexploded bomb.
Uncle Sandbag
was turning back.

I cycled furiously to the next street and hid behind the end wall of a flattened terrace. Uncle Sandbag marched past, fortunately with his eyes straight ahead. Then, just as I was about to give chase, I heard a faint, faint human groan from beneath the rubble.

What could I do? Uncle Sandbag was getting away, but I couldn't ignore the poor soul beneath me. I rode as fast as I could to the warden's post three streets away and blurted out that somebody was buried alive.

Wearily the warden grabbed his hat.

We picked up volunteers along the way and were soon digging into the piles of rafters, brick, plaster and glass that used to be a house.

The groaning seemed to have stopped.

"I should stay clear," said the warden, "if you've never seen a dead body."

Dead body? I was horrified. But I had to watch. The rescue workers turned over the remains of a chair and a leg came into view. Then another . . . then a body, arms, and finally a white, white face, caked in plaster and covered in little red gashes from broken glass.

Suddenly I realised. It was the face of Mr Sanders, who taught at our school!

I watched numbly as they lifted him carefully out, lifeless as a dummy. Then, just as they carried him past me, his white-caked eyes opened. He looked straight at me, confused and blurred.

"Billy Harvey?" he murmured.

"Yes, Sir," I replied, as if he were taking register.

I just hoped my mates never found out I'd saved a teacher.

Mr Stokes the warden congratulated me when the rescue was over. He said I could make a useful messenger boy for the air raid patrol. I said I'd think about it. I couldn't tell him I was on a more important mission.

"He was lucky to be alive," said Mr Stokes. "We pulled out a whole family last time. All dead. It's no darn good hiding under a table if a bomb comes through your blasted roof."

"Wh-what do you think people should do?" I asked.

"Get an Anderson shelter," said Mr Stokes. "And if you ain't got an Anderson, get out of the East End."

We hadn't got an Anderson shelter. According to Gassy Cook, an Anderson shelter was a load of corrugated iron which the council delivered  to your front door. You dug a hole in the back garden and sunk it there. According to Gassy Cook, it then filled with water and you sat there knee-deep all night. But at least you had a chance of surviving if a bomb hit your house.

I decided I wanted to survive.

"Mum," I said, as soon as I got home, "I think we should move."

"Don't be silly," said Mum.

Mum really believed the government would protect us if the bombers came again. But I was starting to agree with Grandad. The government didn't really care if we lived or died.

"Is Uncle back?" I asked, changing the subject.

"Yes," said Mum. "He's been up in the bedroom for ages."

I was off like a rocket up the stairs. Maybe this time I'd catch him.

No such luck. Uncle Sandbag was calmly sitting on the bed reading a newspaper.

He gave me a little smile which convinced
me he'd just radioed Germany. That's it,
I thought to myself. The bombers will be
back tonight.

4

Caught in the Act

I wasn't wrong. The second night of
bombing was every bit as bad as the first.
Once again the East End copped it, and if
anything, our anti-aircraft fire was even
weaker. It even crossed my mind that Nazi
spies were manning the guns.

By morning we were shattered. But
it was Monday, and that meant work,
and school. If you didn't go to work, you
didn't get paid, and if you didn't go to
school, you got ten good stripes from Mr
Morgan's cane.

The playground was buzzing with
stories and souvenirs. Jimmy Hayes had
shrapnel, Tommy Jacobs had cartridge
cases, and Harold Green had this long
metal tube. Mr Morgan got very excited

about this and shouted "You Stupid Boy". He said it was an incendiary bomb – that's the type that starts fires. The only fire Harold felt was the one in the seat of his pants from Mr Morgan's cane.

For all the big talk, you could tell kids were shaken by things they'd seen. When the register was taken, every time someone was missing, it went very quiet. Still, we could always pretend they'd just moved away, or got injured, like Mr Sanders.

Halfway through the afternoon the sirens went, and we all filed down to the school shelter. I took the chance to tell Gassy Cook all about Uncle Sandbag, his suspicious behaviour, and his mysterious cabinet.

As always, Gassy had the answer. "I'll pick the lock," he said.

"Can you pick locks?" I asked.

"Sure I can!"

So it was that Gassy followed me home that afternoon. We told Mum I was helping Gassy with his homework, then tiptoed up to the bedroom.

Good news. No sign of uncle. I kept watch through a little hole in the blackout and Gassy got to work.

"Hmm" he said. "Nothing special."

Gassy took out a thin piece of wire, poked it in the keyhole and felt around a bit.

"Shouldn't take a minute."

Unfortunately Gassy was wrong. It took several minutes, and still he wasn't getting anywhere.

"Are you *sure* you know how to pick locks?" I asked.

"Course!"

Time wore on. I became nervous.

"Tell you what," said Gassy, "I'll try another way."

With that, Gassy whipped out a
screwdriver and started undoing the whole
lock. It would look the same when he was
done, he said.

The screws began to loosen and my
stomach began to tighten.

Suddenly there was a footfall on the
stair. Not Grandad's – too heavy for that.
Not Dad's – he'd gone to volunteer as a
firefighter.

I held my breath.

Then the door flew open and my worst
nightmare came true.

"What the hell are you doing!?"

I had never seen Uncle Sandbag look so frightening. The veins on his neck bulged and his eyes were aflame with fury.

"We wanted . . . to borrow some screws," I said, lamely.

Uncle Sandbag swiftly shut the door, then took one great stride into the room, snatching the screwdriver from Gassy and covering the cabinet with his big baggy body.

"Have you opened this?" he stormed.

"No, Uncle, honest!"

"What have you seen?" he snapped.

"Nothing! Nothing!"

Both Gassy and I were crouched in terror on the bed. I was sure Uncle Sandbag had a gun in that strange case he always carried. Or maybe a knife in his belt. Either way, he looked ready to kill us.

"You listen to me!" he said.

"That cabinet's mine, and everything
inside it! *No one else's!* Understand?"

"Yes, Uncle" I replied meekly.

There was no way I'd risk touching
that cabinet again.

5

A Race For Safety

And that might have been the end of the
story. I might have been none the wiser
about Uncle Sandbag. But it wasn't the
end of the Blitz, far from it, and that night
the bombers were back. Ruby was working,
Dad was with the firefighters, and the rest

of us were back under the kitchen table.

Then, suddenly, there was an almighty BOOM like the Earth had cracked.

"They've hit us!" yelled Mum.

We sat stock still in shock. You could smell the fear, and most of it seemed to be in my brother Roy's shorts.

"Must be next door," said Grandad, noticing that we were all still alive.

Suddenly Mum started pushing us out from under the table. "Come on!" she said.

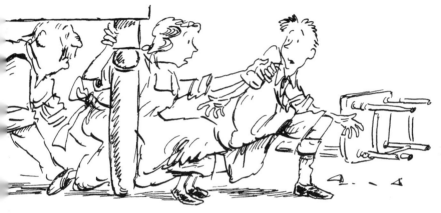

"Where are we going?" I asked.

"Somewhere safe," said Mum.

There was no time to take anything with us. The whole family was bundled out of the front door, right into the middle of the most terrible sound-and-light show you could imagine. Searchlights swept the sky, anti-aircraft shells exploded in the air, giant bombers droned overhead, and the

whole landscape was lit by fires and explosions. It almost seemed unreal, but the danger of death was real enough.

We ran through the streets, hardly daring to stop for breath. We knew there were shelters, but we had no idea what we'd find there. Some said the shelters were no safer than your own home, and that you'd be lucky to find one with a roof. Others said they were like visions of hell, thousands of people crammed together and not one toilet.

As we reached the main road, however, we could see there was one place to shelter we hadn't thought of – the underground station. There was a crowd of people there, and as we got closer we could see a line of troops holding them back. The atmosphere was dangerous and panicky and tempers were frayed.

A railway official was frantically pointing at a poster on the wall:

UNDERGROUND STATIONS MUST NOT BE USED AS AIR RAID SHELTERS.

But whatever the reasons the man was giving, they weren't going down well with the East Enders. The crowd surged, the troops pushed back, and Grandad took us smartly to one side.

"Has everyone got three ha'pence?" he asked.

We nodded.

"Follow me," said Grandad. He made his way past the edge of the crowd to the ticket office, bought a ticket, and set off down to the trains. We followed. Reaching the platform, Grandad selected a nice spot and sat himself down.

"Now try and move me," he said.

Soon dozens more were copying
Grandad's example. The platform was
starting to look like a street party. I looked
on enviously as other families arrived with
blankets, flasks and sandwiches.

It was a strange and magical
atmosphere down in that tube station.
Everybody got talking, and of course we'd
all been through the same things.

Soon people were sharing the few things they'd got – cushions, cigarettes, sandwiches. It really made you feel you belonged. You were an East Ender.

Uncle Sandbag, on the other hand, seemed to find all this very difficult. He sat at a distance from everybody else and kept himself to himself.

Needless to say, people noticed.

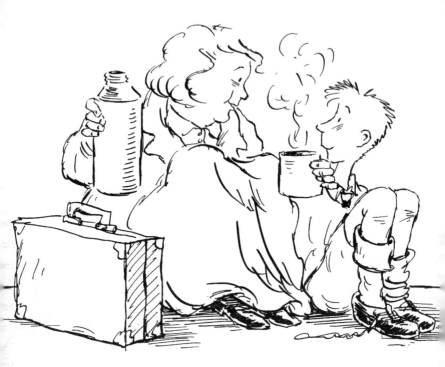

"Wouldn't your uncle like a nice hot cup of tea?" asked the woman next to me, "or a sandwich?"

Uncle Sandbag half turned. I knew he was starving, and like I said, his motto was Pig for Victory.

"Sandwich, love?" asked the woman. "We're all in the same boat."

Suddenly Uncle Sandbag jumped to
his feet. "I've forgotten something," he
mumbled. Without another word he
marched back up the steps towards
the surface.

"Sandy!" cried Mum. "Where are you going?"

But there was no further sign of Uncle Sandbag.

6

A Guilty Surprise

The next thing I remember was being
elbowed in the ribs by my brother.

"Come on, Bill," he said. "The all-
clear's gone."

I rubbed my eyes and looked around.
"Where's Uncle Sandbag?" I asked.

"He never came back," replied my brother.

We made our way back up the steps, past the ticket office, and into the light. Things were quiet now, apart from the occasional ambulance. We sloped back home, wondering what we would find.

Just as we were about to turn our corner, Mrs Harrison from across the road rushed over to Mum and put her arms round her.

"Mildred!" she said. "We thought you were under the rubble."

"What rubble?" said Mum, almost silently.

"But didn't you know? You were hit last night."

I had strange mixed feelings of relief and sickness.

"We thought you were all under there," said Mrs Harrison, "once they found the first body."

A chill went through me. Uncle Sandbag!

Suddenly we found ourselves running, down a street we hardly recognised, to a house which no longer existed. The warden showed us the spot they dug out our uncle.

There, amongst the bricks and rafters,
lay a certain small cabinet,
the door blasted
from its hinges.

I gasped. The cabinet was stuffed with
every foodstuff you could imagine – butter,
tins of fruit, sugar, flour, even chocolate.
There were fags as well.

"I think someone's been working the
black market," said the warden, sternly.

"We knew nothing," said Mum, stunned.

"Funny thing," said the warden, "but
his pockets were filled with the stuff as well.
Must have been on his way somewhere."

Yes, I thought. Back to the tube, to share it out with the rest of the people there.

For all the bad things I'd thought about Uncle Sandbag, I knew that was what he was doing.

"Is he. . . dead?" I asked.

The warden looked at me long and hard. "Not till I get my hands on him," he replied.

"I'll be right behind you," said Mum.

I said nothing. I remembered Grandad saying there was a little bit of good in everyone.

Looked like the Blitz had finally brought it out of Uncle Sandbag.

London at War

The Blitz

The Blitz got its
name from "Blitzkrieg" –
German for "lightning war". This described
how quickly countries were attacked and how
much damage was done to them.

Mass bombing first took place in the Spanish
Civil War. In 1937, 43 planes dropped 100,000
tonnes of explosives on the town of Guernica.
The world was shocked. Some people began to
believe that wars would be won by bombing cities
rather than fighting.

A Surprise Attack

The Blitz began on 7 September 1940 and ended
on 10 May 1941. London was bombed for 76

nights in a row, apart from just one night. About 43,000 people died; two million homes were damaged or destroyed; one and a half million people were made homeless.

The government did not expect the Blitz. The shelters they provided were unsafe, unclean and too few in number. The main targets were homes and factories. When factories were hit, they stopped producing goods. This meant there was a shortage of everyday things like soap, clothes and food. Hitler wanted to make the British people give up hope by destroying their homes and cutting off supplies. However, people's spirits did not collapse as badly as Hitler hoped.

British Bombers

The Blitz happened at a time when Britain was doing poorly in the war. The government believed it would be followed by an invasion. But the Germans had their hands full in Russia, and after 10th of May, switched their main efforts there. Bombing raids did continue, but they were much less frequent.

In fact, the bombing of Germany by British planes was far more severe than the bombing of Britain. In one night, more than 60,000 civilians died in the city of Dresden, where incendiary bombs created a huge firestorm.

The Prisoner

by
Penny McKinlay

Illustrations by Greg Gormley

1

The Enemy Surrenders

"Rat-tat-tat-tat-tat!" The sound of
machine-gun fire shattered the dreamy
September warmth of the wheat-field.
"Come out, now, with your hands up!"
shouted Bob. "I've got you covered!"

He waved his wooden stick

threateningly at the
haystack. He knew Jack
was hiding behind it.

"Rat-tat-
tat-tat!" he
screamed again.
"You're dead
now, Jack!
I've won!"

Silence.
Nothing moved. Then:
"STOP THIS, STOP, STOP!"

The dark body of a man hurled itself
from the top of the haystack and pinned Bob

to the ground. Terrified,
Bob screamed to Jack
for help. The stranger
pushed his face close to
his, spitting out strange
words. It was a twisted,

wild face, streaked with tears. Bob cried
out in pain as the man crushed him
against the sharp stubble
of the cut wheat.

Jack jumped
on to the man's
back, trying to pull
him off Bob. "Get
off, get off, you're
hurting him!"

The
man quite
suddenly let
go of Bob and sank back on his knees,
sobbing. Bob scrambled to his feet and
he and Jack stood watching, bewildered.
They had never seen a man cry before.
He wasn't so frightening now.

"I sorry, sorry." They were the first
words Bob could understand. "Is bad

game you play with guns! You not understand."

"He's one of those Italian prisoners," whispered Jack. "From the prisoner of war camp. He's working for my dad on the farm, getting the harvest in."

Bob stared, backed away. He shivered. It was as if Jack had just told him the man was the devil.

So this was the enemy, one of the men Dad had been fighting until he was taken prisoner and locked up in a prison camp.

Now Dad couldn't come home until the end of the war.

Bob couldn't remember when there hadn't been a war on. Five years, his mum said, but that was half Bob's life. This war that made his mum so sad and tired-looking. This war that meant nothing but horrible food. This war that meant hardly any sweets. This war that had taken his dad away. He didn't really believe the war would ever end, but he didn't say that to his mum. He didn't want to upset her.

He looked back at the man. He was quieter now, staring at them. There was something about his eyes that bothered Bob. Then he remembered when he and his dad had found a fox cowering exhausted in the lane. Bob had

never forgotten the animal's eyes, pleading for help. Moments later the hunters and the fox-hounds swept round the corner and the fox was killed.

Bob suddenly realised that this man, this enemy, was scared of them.

"I'm going to tell my dad." Jack was the first to speak. "You'll be punished, they won't let you out of the camp again."

"Please, no tell!" cried the man. He struggled to find the right English words to explain. "Bang! Bang! The shooting, for you is a game. For me, is real. My friends, they all died. I cannot forget."

Just then came a shout.

"Mario, Mario!" It was Jack's dad. Bob called him Uncle Leonard, but he wasn't a real uncle. Like their mums and dads, Jack and Bob had grown up together in the village. But when the war came Bob's dad had to go away to fight. Now Bob secretly felt jealous of Jack because his dad didn't have to go to war. He was a farmer and he was needed to stay at home and grow food for everyone, 'Digging for Victory!' like it said on all the posters.

When the Italian heard Uncle Leonard calling, he jumped up and ran back to join the other men hard at work harvesting. He shouted back over his shoulder, "Please, no tell. I sorry."

The two friends picked up their sticks

and walked silently back towards the farm.
Neither of them felt like shooting each
other any more.

"Don't tell, Jack," Bob said suddenly.

"Why not?" argued Jack. "He hurt
you." Bob stopped. He didn't know why.
He kept seeing that fox, those eyes.

"I just feel sorry for him, I suppose."
Jack stared at him.

"Sorry for an Italian!" he exploded.
"They're the enemy. What if your dad
heard you saying that?" Bob felt tears
pricking behind his eyes. He didn't want
Jack to see, so he broke into a run.

"I've got to get home for my
tea," he shouted back. "I'll see
you tomorrow!" And he took
off across the fields, running
away from all these questions
with no answers.

2

Making Do

Back home, Bob burst into the kitchen to be greeted by the usual smell of cabbage and the unusual sight of a girl standing on a chair, dipping a rag into a jug of brown stuff and rubbing it on her legs.

"What on earth are you doing, Nell?"

"Painting my legs with gravy browning," said Nell, as if it was the most normal thing in the world. Nell was from London, but she was staying with them because she was working in the Land Army, helping on the farm while the men were away in the real army.

"All the girls do it, it makes you look like you've got stockings on. And since there isn't a pair of stockings to be had for love nor money out here in the wilderness, this is the best I can do – I'm going to that dance in the village tonight. Now come here and help. Can you draw in a straight line?"

"What on earth are you doing, Bob?"

cried Mum when she walked into the kitchen. Bob was concentrating on drawing a perfect straight line down the back of Nell's legs. His hand slipped.

"He's drawing the seams in for my stockings, Mrs Gander," said Nell. "Now look, Bob, you'll have to do that bit again."

Mum stared, then laughed. "Now I've seen it all! That's real 'make do and mend', that is! You're right though, Nell, I don't remember the last time I had a pair of stockings." Mum was always talking about 'make do and mend', ideas she got from the wireless and women's magazines about making old things last longer, now new clothes were rationed and hard to get. Bob hadn't had any new clothes for ages, it was all cut-down stuff of his dad's. Not that it bothered him, but he knew that Mum minded not having anything new. He remembered once they had gone to the pictures in town for his birthday. The film was full of ladies dancing in pretty dresses and when they came out he could see tears in her eyes.

"I know it's a wicked thing to cry over when people are dying every day," she sniffed. "But, Bob, I'd give anything to go out dancing with your dad again in a dress like that."

Bob looked at her smiling now. Mum was a lot happier since Nell had come to live with them. Nell made them laugh with her stories about working on the farm.

"What's for supper, Mum?" he asked, not very hopefully.

"Cabbage pie," replied Mum. "With –"

"Plenty of potatoes!" interrupted Nell and Bob together. "Not again!"

Mum looked upset.

"That's all there is," she apologised.

"I queued up for ages at the butcher but there was nothing left. He's promised us something for tomorrow."

"Don't worry, Mum," said Bob quickly. Why couldn't they put cabbage on the ration instead of sweets? He thought how to cheer Mum up. "Nell, tell us about the tomatoes again!"

Nell groaned. "Not that old one!" But as they sat down to eat she told Bob's favourite story again, about the day she started in the Land Army. "I'd never been near a farm in my life! Never been out of London, in fact," she began. "I only went for the Land Army because I liked the

uniform! Anyway, first day, your Uncle Leonard, he takes me over to the tomatoes. 'Here you are, love,' he says. 'Start with something easy. You can shoot the tomatoes.'

And I say, 'But I haven't got a gun!' I didn't realise he just meant take the new shoots off the plants to stop them growing too fast – I didn't have a clue!"

Laughing took Bob's mind off the cabbage pie. It also took his mind off the Italian prisoner, but not for long. He tried to push the thoughts away all evening, scared to tell Mum. How would she feel about him talking to the enemy?

"You're very quiet, love," she said that night as she tucked him into bed. "Everything all right?"

"Yes, Mum, fine."

But in the darkness his old nightmare came back. It was always the same, his dad being beaten while he stood watching, frozen to the spot. Only this time he could see the face of the man hurting his dad. It was the Italian prisoner.

"Stop it, stop it!" he shouted, and woke himself up. Mum came running in.

"What is it, Bob?" And then it

all came tumbling out while Mum hugged him safe against the rough wool of Dad's old overcoat that she used as a dressing-gown. He was a little boy again. He told her all about the Italian, and she went very quiet.

"Are you cross with me, Mum?" asked Bob.

"No, of course not, Bob." But she looked shocked.

"Trouble is, I felt sorry for him and Jack said Dad would be angry if he knew."

Mum was silent. Her face flickered with feelings.

"Well, Dad's a prisoner, too, Bob, so perhaps he would understand how the Italian feels. He's just another human being, after all. And we aren't even at war with Italy any more. They're on our side now." Finally, as if she had suddenly found the right answer, she said, "Anyway, I'd like to think, wherever Dad is, that someone's being kind to him. So I think we should be kind to the Italian." Bob smiled at her, relieved. "Now, what about a bit of a snack? I've made a cake with a real egg Jack's mum gave me. Come on."

Downstairs they sat together with big cups of tea and the delicious cake, not made with the usual carrots or potato.

Bob snuggled close inside Dad's overcoat. It was full of his dad's smell, and he suddenly missed him terribly. The sobs rose up from his heart and he couldn't keep them down. Mum wrapped the coat round him and held him tight until he could speak.

"This war's never going to end, is it, Mum? Tell me the truth."

Mum stared at him.

"Oh, Bob, it is going to end. We're beating the Germans everywhere now." She paused. "I suppose for you it seems to have gone on for ever."

Bob nodded miserably.

"Look," said Mum. She pulled the map of Europe out of the drawer. Then

she pinned it up on the wall.

"I put this away when the war was going so badly. Let's put it back up, and after

150

we've listened to the news on the wireless every day we'll move the little flags for each army. Then you'll see, we are winning now. And how about this!" Mum threw open the

thick black curtains that stopped the lights showing to the enemy aircraft so they couldn't drop bombs on them.

"Mum!" cried Bob, terrified. "What about the blackout! You'll get into trouble!"

"No, I won't," replied Mum. "Come and see!"

Bob went over to the window. The village street, pitch black at night throughout the war, was lit up like fairyland. "The street lights are back on, Bob," said Mum, smiling. "It's the beginning of the end."

3

"Ciao!"

Bob didn't see the Italian again for a while, until one cold Saturday morning in the autumn Mum announced they had to help Uncle Leonard on the farm.

"Oh, Mum!" groaned Bob. He'd planned to play football as usual.

"Bob!" Mum was really angry.
"Everyone has to do their bit to help,
that's what's got us through this war!"

And so it was that Bob ended up in a
field digging up turnips next to the Italian.
He kept his head down, embarrassed.

"Ciao!" the Italian
said suddenly.

"Where?" said
Bob, startled. He
looked round.
He thought he
said 'cow'.
The Italian
laughed. It was
a nice laugh.

"Not cow –
'ciao!'" he repeated. "In my
country, means 'hello'."

He stretched out his hand, and Bob

* 'Ciao' is Italian for 'hello' - say it 'chow'

shook it politely. The skin was
rough and cracked.

"You need gloves,"
said Bob.

"Yes. England is
too cold. Not like
Italy!" His English
had got better.
"How old are you?"

"Ten,"
said Bob.

"My little
brother, Roberto,
he is ten, like you," said the Italian.

"That's my name, Robert," said Bob,
surprised.

"I am Mario," said the Italian.
Then he added quietly, "Roberto is like
you, he loves football. I miss him, and
my mother."

Bob plucked up courage to ask a question. "Where do you live, in England I mean? Are you locked up in prison?"

"No, we live in a big camp. Is not bad, better than when we were fighting. Since Italy stop fighting with Germans and join British side, some Italians, they leave camp and live on farms. Is better, I think. More like home."

They talked all afternoon. Mario seemed glad to talk about his family. Bob watched sadly in the cold dusk as Mario climbed into the back of the lorry to go back to the prison camp.

He and Jack went into the warm farm kitchen. Mum and Auntie May had made a big tea and Uncle Leonard was already tucking in.

"Auntie May, why can't Mario live here instead of at the camp?" Bob suddenly burst out. "He misses his family – he'd be much happier here!"

"Bob!" scolded his mum. "That's none of our business!"

But Bob couldn't stop.

"Please, Uncle Leonard," he begged.

"Dad's a prisoner too – it's like someone being kind to him."

Uncle Leonard looked doubtful.

"I don't know, Bob, it's a big responsibility. What if he disappears, tries to go back to Italy? I'll get the blame."

"I'll keep an eye on him," promised Bob.

"I'll think about it," was all Uncle Leonard would say.

4
The Camp

Uncle Leonard did think about it. Next Saturday he drove up to Bob's cottage in his truck. Jack was with him.

"Hop in," he said. "We're going to fetch your Italian friend."

The camp was a big field with tall

fences, topped with barbed wire. Uncle
Leonard stopped at the gate, and the guards
waved him through. While he was sorting
things out with a man in uniform, Bob and
Jack stared around. It was very bleak, with
thick mud everywhere. There were long rows
of huts and inside Bob got a glimpse of long
rows of narrow beds. No wonder Mario
missed home.

Then Mario climbed in beside them. He

PRISONER CAMP
Nº 3402

was smiling, and his face looked suddenly quite different.

"Thank you," he said simply.

Mario soon settled in, in a spare room at the top of the farmhouse. Sometimes at weekends he played football with the boys, and even Jack admitted he was 'all right really'.

One morning, about six weeks before Christmas, Mum was round at the farm.

She and Auntie May had put their points together to get enough dried fruit for a proper Christmas cake. Everyone crowded round the bowl to stir the cake and make a wish. Bob wished for Dad to come home soon.

"No secret what we're all wishing for," said Auntie May. "Let's hope this is our last war-time Christmas."

Mario and Nell came in. They had been out working together.

"Come and have a wish, you two!" said Mum.

Nell smiled at Mario shyly, and they took it in turns to wish.

All afternoon delicious cake smells wafted through the open window. Later

Bob saw the cake cooling on the window-sill.

Suddenly there was a scream and a squawk, and the ginger tom-cat came tearing out as if his tail was on fire. Auntie May chased after him with the kitchen knife in her hand.

Bob and Jack went inside. There was the cake with a big hole in the middle.

"But cats don't eat cake!" said Bob.

"Tell Ginger that!" said Auntie May.

Nell and Mario rushed in. Nell gasped: "What a waste of rations!"

"No, not waste!" said Mario firmly.

He took the knife from Auntie May and cut away the edges of the hole. Then he took the pretend marzipan Mum and Auntie May had made and filled in the gap. They all watched in amazement as his fingers worked, shaping the marzipan on top of the cake into all sorts of wonderful flowers, birds and animals. By the time he had finished, the cake was a work of art.

"Why, it's lovely, Mario," said Mum.

"I love to cook," said Mario smiling. "In Italy, is my job."

Jack looked as though Mario had said he could fly.

"Men don't cook," he said bluntly.

"In my country, men cook," said Mario. And he described the food in Italy. His whole face lit up as he talked of things they had never heard of, spaghetti and pizzas and many other strange-sounding things. "One day, I will make these things for you, after the war."

5

The Runaway

The weeks before Christmas were endless
– it was a bitterly cold winter that seemed
to go on and on. At last Christmas Eve
came, as snowy as a scene on a Christmas
card. In the morning a thick envelope
arrived, with a letter each for Mum and

Bob from Dad in the prison camp. Bob liked to read Dad's letters in private, so he could hear his voice in his head. He ran down to the barn. He climbed the huge wall of straw and snuggled down.

Dad's letter was full of stuff about playing football in the prison camp, and he asked about Jack, and school. He never complained, but he sounded so sad.

"I do miss you, Bob, and your mum," he wrote. "This war seems to go on for ever. But it will end, and soon we will all be together again. I love you, son. Dad."

The sudden sound of a man weeping sent a shiver through Bob. For a moment he thought he was hearing Dad, hundreds of miles away. After the first shock Bob realised the weeping was coming from inside the barn. He peered down. In the half-light he could make out Mario, his body hunched into a ball of misery.

"Mamma!" Bob could hear him

whispering. "Mamma!" Bob did not know
what to do. Mario suddenly stood up,
dashing tears from his eyes, and
stormed out.

Bob quickly slid down the straw and
made for the door. A piece of paper was
trapped underneath. He picked it up.
It was a letter, but he couldn't read it. It
was in Italian.

Bob peered out into the snowy
farmyard, then ducked back in. Mario
was wheeling Uncle Leonard's bike out

from the shed. He had a kit bag on his back, and as Bob peeped out again, he cycled off, the wheels sliding in the slushy snow.

He was running away!

Bob stood in the doorway, horrified. He felt as frozen as Jack's snowman. He promised Uncle Leonard he'd keep an eye on Mario. Now Mario was running away and Uncle Leonard would get into trouble.

Then he saw Jack coming out of the back door, wrapped up warm with his wellies and scarf and hat.

"Jack!" he hissed. "Jack, over here!" He
put his fingers to his lips. Jack trudged over
and Bob pulled him quickly inside. "Mario's
run away!" Bob announced. Jack's eyes wen
round as gobstoppers. "He must have had
bad news from Italy – look!" Bob showed
Jack the letter. "What shall we do?"

"Get Nell!" said Jack.

"Why Nell?" demanded Bob.

"Because they're sweet on each other,
stupid. My mum said," replied Jack. "Nell
will get him to come back, you'll see."

Nell was having a few days off from the farm for Christmas, so the boys struggled back down the snowy lane to Bob's house. They watched through the window until Mum left Nell alone in the kitchen. She was getting ready to go out that night, her hair tightly curled in twists of paper.

"What are you up to, you two?" she said crossly when she came to the door. "Playing German spies again?" But her face changed as they explained. "I'm coming," she said. "Wait for me in the farmyard."

When she joined them she was in her thick Land Army coat and hat and heavy boots. She shouted to Uncle Leonard: "I'm taking the tractor to check on those sheep, Len!" and then swung herself up, tiny behind the big wheel. The boys started to climb on after her. "Oh, no you don't!" she said firmly. "You've got to follow the tracks!"

Off they went along the lane, the two boys following the narrow tyre marks, wider sometimes where the bike had slipped in the snow.

"He's fallen off a few times," said Jack. "Trust an Italian not to know you can't ride a bike in the snow!"

But Mario hadn't given up. Mile after mile the strange procession crept along, and soon it started to get dark. Nell put the headlamps on, but they could hardly see the bicycle tracks.

At last they came to a crossroads. The tracks disappeared.

"He must be heading for the coast, to try and get a ship home," said Bob.

"But which way is the coast?" cried Nell.

There were no road signs – they had been taken down at the start of the war to confuse the Germans if they invaded.

"I'm hungry," said Jack. "Let's go home."

Nell got down and walked ahead, shining a torch. She wouldn't give up. Then suddenly the boys saw someone lurch out of the hedge.

"Nell!"

"Oh, Mario, we were so worried!" Nell cried as they hugged each other. "Boys!" she shouted. "He's here, we've found him."

Uncle Leonard's bike lay with a twisted wheel where Mario had hit a stone in the

snow. Together the boys loaded it into the
trailer, while Nell helped the shivering Mario
on to the tractor.

"My mother, Nell," he was saying, over
and over. "She is sick, I must go – there is
no one to look after her."

"Mario," said Nell gently. "You can't go,
you have to stay in England until the war
ends. She'll be all right, you'll see."

"And what about my dad?" piped up
Jack. "You'll get him into trouble, too!"

"Anyway, we'd miss you," said Bob.

"Besides," said Nell. "You said you'd take me to the Christmas Eve dance tonight." She pulled her Land Army hat off. "Look - here's me with my curlers in, chasing over England after my date!"

They all laughed, perched high up there on the tractor in the snow. And Mario gave Nell a kiss.

"Yeuch!" said Bob and Jack together.

6

Christmas

"Happy Christmas, sleepy-head!" It was
Mum, kissing him awake. For the first time
in his life, Bob had to be woken up on
Christmas morning, he was so tired after
the trek the day before. But at least they
had managed to get back without any of

the grown-ups noticing there was anything
wrong.

"Last Christmas of the war, Bob!"
Mum said.

"And last Christmas without Dad!"
added Bob. They smiled at each other.

Nell was already downstairs, and they
all sat down to open presents together.

As usual it was Nell that made them all laugh and forget about Dad not being there. She handed Mum a heavy round present.

"Read the label!" said Nell.

"Bottled stockings?" Mum pulled the wrapping off. Inside was a bottle of gravy browning.

"Now you can paint your legs too!"

But after they stopped laughing, Nell pulled out a smaller softer parcel and handed it to Mum.

"This is your real present," she said. "Thanks for making me part of the family." Inside was a pair of real stockings.

"Nell! However did you manage to get these?"

"Never mind that," replied Nell. "My mum can get a few things in London you can't get here – you can wear them for that first dance when your hubby gets back!"

They were all going to the farm for Christmas lunch.

"Mum," said Bob, after breakfast, "will Mario be having lunch with us all?"

"Yes, I suppose so," said Mum. "Why?"

"Could we make him one of those pizza things he was talking about, to make him feel more at home?" Mum and Nell looked at each other.

"Why not?" said Mum. "Let's have a go."

And so it was that they spent Christmas morning 1944 cooking Italian food in that small kitchen in the English countryside – or trying to, at least.

"He said bread at the bottom," said Bob. So they cut a thick slice of bread.

"And tomatoes," said Mum. "I've got some bottled tomatoes from the summer." So they spread some tomatoes on the top.

"Then cheese," said Nell. She got out her week's cheese ration – she got extra because she was in the Land Army – and cut it up into small pieces. Then they put it in the oven for a few minutes. They all stared at it doubtfully when they took it out.

"It's just cheese on toast with tomatoes," said Nell, flatly.

"Well, we did what he said," said Mum. "It's obviously what they like over there in foreign parts." And they put it in a dish and carried it carefully to the farm.

At lunchtime they were gathered round the table in the dining room, the room that was kept for special occasions. Mario was sitting next to Nell, and Bob was sitting beside Jack. Mario looked much happier today. He bent his head and whispered something to Nell and Bob saw him squeeze her hand. She smiled back at

him, and then blushed when she noticed Bob watching.

She turned and whispered to Bob. "It's good news, Bob. Someone brought another letter over from the camp this morning – Mario's mother is much better."

Just then Auntie May called Bob through into the kitchen. She handed him the 'pizza' on a serving dish.

"Here you are, lad, since it was your

idea. I'll take the turkey – you take the pizza!" And in they went together, carrying the Christmas lunch, one English, one Italian.

Mario's face was full of amazement when Bob put the pizza down in front of him.

"Is wonderful!" he said, and Bob could see tears in his eyes. "Thank you, thank you. One day you come to Italy, and I cook for you, when the war is over!"

"Here's to that!" said Uncle Leonard, and he lifted his glass. "Let's drink to when the war is over!"

And together they drank a toast to the end of the war, when everyone would finally be at home.

Britain in the Second World War

Britain and France declared war on Germany in September 1939, but by the middle of 1940 Britain

was left to fight alone after France was occupied by Germany. At this time Italy joined the German side. For a long time everyone was afraid that Germany would invade Britain too. Many British towns and cities were bombed and many people were killed.

In 1941 the Soviet Union and America joined the British side against Germany and Italy, and together they planned how to defeat the Germans. They were known as 'the Allies'.

Things looked very bad for the Allies for a long time, until they defeated the Germans and Italians in North Africa in the middle of 1943. Soon afterwards Allied troops landed in Italy and by September Italy made peace.

At last, in June 1944, on D-Day, thousands of Allied troops crossed the Channel from England to France and began to drive the German army out of France. At the same time the German army was being pushed back from Italy and Eastern Europe.

Prisoners of War

In this story, Mario is a made-up character, but there were many Italian and German prisoners in Britain during the Second World War. There were over 600 prisoner-of-war (POW) camps all over Britain, where enemy soldiers were taken after they had been captured. They were well treated in the camps, although, as for everyone else in Britain, the food was dull and not always very plentiful. Life was also dull, and prisoners played cards or made board games to pass the time. In some camps they formed orchestras and choirs, and performed plays to keep themselves busy. Many played football.

Some German and Italian prisoners of war worked on farms, because many farm workers had gone to fight in the war. After Italy surrendered to Britain and her allies, Italian prisoners had more freedom, although they were not allowed to go back to Italy until after the war. Some Italians went to live on farms where they were working. Many made friends with British people, and some fell in love with local girls.

Rationing

Soon after the war started everyone was issued with ration books. This meant they were allowed a fixed amount of certain foods depending on how many points they had. There was not as much food to go round, because many ships bringing food across the sea were sunk by German submarines. During the war many foods were rationed – bacon, ham, sugar, butter, meat, tea, margarine, cheese, cooking fat, jam, marmalade, treacle, syrup, eggs, milk and sweets. Lots of foods were hardly available at all – like bananas.

Everyone was encouraged to grow as much food as they could at home, so there were always plenty of vegetables. People living on farms, like Jack's family, could get food more easily than people living in towns.

About the authors

JON BLAKE

I first decided to be a writer at the age of six. I got my first book published when I was thirty-one. My favourite subjects at school were History and English, so I suppose it was natural for me to write historical stories. I research my stories thoroughly, and try to write from the point of view of ordinary people. I also try to make them funny, but there are serious points within them. You can probably guess from *Sid's War* that I don't like snobbery.

PENNY MCKINLAY

I've written several historical novels for children, mostly about the Second World War. Many of the characters and events in my war-time books are based on real interviews I did for television programmes with men, women and children who lived through the war. I also read lots of letters written by people parted by war – often written to mothers and fathers, sisters and brothers they never saw again. The stories they told me were so vivid, so painful, and sometimes, so exciting, that it still made them cry to remember, even though they happened so many years ago.

Acknowledgements

Franklin Watts would like to thank
the following for the use of copyright
material in this collection.

All books cited are originally
published in the *Sparks* series
by Franklin Watts.

SID'S WAR
Text © Jon Blake 1998
Illustrations © Kate Sheppard1988

THE SANDBAG SECRET
Text © Jon Blake 1997
Illustrations © Franklin Watts 1997

THE PRISONER
Text © Penny McKinlay 1997
Illustrations © Franklin Watts 1997

If you enjoyed these
bomb-blasted stories, why not
read some hair-raising adventures
about some nasty parts of
Victorian life?

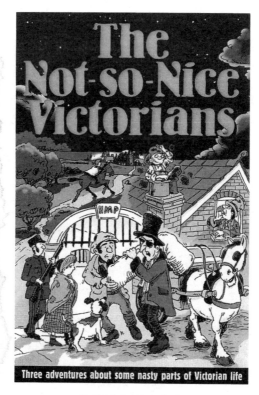

0 7496 6316 2